And the Winner Is...

To my wife, Simone, and my children, Najee, Italia, Samaria, and Nina.
Thank you for your undying support and understanding. — LLCJ

This book is dedicated to Carl Bedigian, our good friend and a true hero. — JibJab

ISBN 0-439-38911-9

Text and illustrations copyright © 2002 by ONE GAZILLION, INC.

All rights reserved.   Published by Scholastic Inc., 557 Broadway, New York, NY 10012.
SCHOLASTIC, CARTWHEEL BOOKS, and associated logos are trademarks and/or registered trademarks of Scholastic Inc.

Library of Congress Cataloging-in-Publication Data available

The text type was set in Rockwell Bold Condensed.
Book design by Steven Scott.

12 11 10 9 8 7 6 5 4 3 2 1   02 03 04 05 06

Printed in China   62
First Scholastic printing, September 2002

HIPKIDHOP

And the Winner Is...

By LL Cool J

Illustrated by JibJab Media

SCHOLASTIC INC.

New York   Toronto   London   Auckland   Sydney   Mexico City   New Delhi   Hong Kong   Buenos Aires

**Remember when you won
how you laughed at your competition?
From that day forward
victory became your mission.**

Shaking hands was merely a formality.

Winning was your only reality.

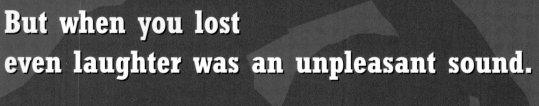

But when you lost
even laughter was an unpleasant sound.

Your smile became heavy,
then it fell to the ground.

Your head hung low, you had a feeling deep down,
That anyone who smiled at you thought you were a clown.

You felt angry and frustrated
with no self-respect.

When you heard the winners cheering,
you wished they understood,

How hurt you felt
when they felt so good.

Here's what to do when you get
that sensation.
Close your eyes and say this out loud
to find inspiration:

I never ever give up.
I never give up.

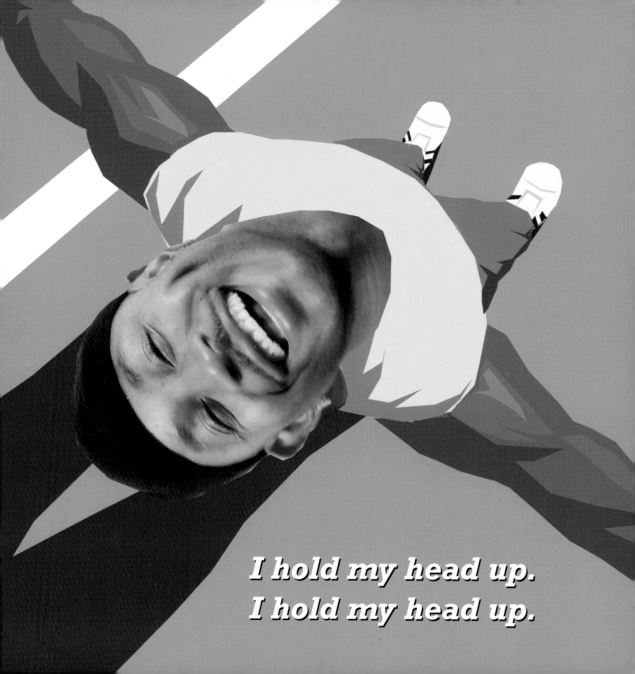

I hold my head up.
I hold my head up.

Now when it's your turn to win,
and you *will* get the chance,

Will you accept gracefully
or do a taunting victory dance?

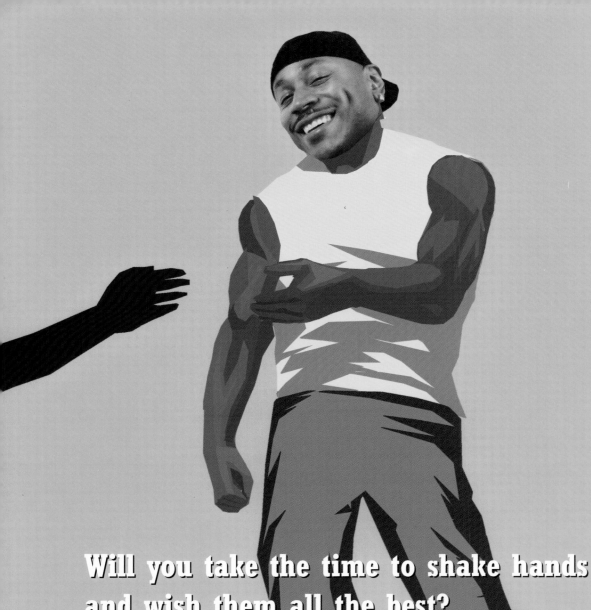

Will you take the time to shake hands and wish them all the best?

Or will you do everything
to make them feel they're less?

When you're a winner,
as you've been before,

Remember to walk with humility,
and never be a loser who's sore.

Winning and losing is
only a test.
Be gracious either way and
you will *always*
be the best.

**Believe in yourself,
have fun and be true.**

**Give it your all.
Be proud! Be you!**

And remember:
NEVER GIVE UP!
HOLD YOUR HEAD UP!